Pizazz

VS. Perfecto

PiZAZZ

vs. Perfecto

Sophy Henn

ALADDIN

New York London Toronto Sydney New Delhi

ALADDIN

An imprint of Simon & Schuster Children's Publishing Division

1230 Avenue of the Americas, New York, New York 10020

First Aladdin paperback edition December 2021

Copyright © 2021 by Sophy Henn

Originally published in Great Britain in 2021 by Simon & Schuster UK

Also available in an Aladdin hardcover edition.

All rights reserved, including the right of reproduction in whole or in part in any form.

ALADDIN and related logo are registered trademarks of Simon & Schuster, Inc.

For information about special discounts for bulk purchases, please contact Simon & Schuster Special Sales at 1-866-506-1949 or business@simonandschuster.com.

The Simon & Schuster Speakers Bureau can bring authors to your live event.

For more information or to book an event contact the Simon & Schuster Speakers Bureau at 1-866-248-3049 or visit our website at www.simonspeakers.com.

The illustrations for this book were rendered digitally.

The text of this book was set in New Clarendon MT.

Manufactured in the United States of America 1021 OFF

2 4 6 8 10 9 7 5 3 1

Library of Congress Control Number 2021940846

ISBN 978-1-5344-9249-3 (hc)

ISBN 978-1-5344-9248-6 (pbk)

ISBN 978-1-5344-9250-9 (ebook)

A (little) bit about me . . .

Hi. I'm **PIZAZZ**, I'm 9½ (FINALLY!), and I am **SUPER**. You might think that I'm a bigheaded **SHOW-OFF** pants for saying that, but you would be completely wrong. COMPLETELY. I mean, I am **SUPER**, but not in the way you probably think.

You see, I am definitely *not* fantastic, or particularly great, and I'm barely terrific, but I am

SUPER. **SUPER SUPER.**

UGH. What I'm trying to say is . . .

. . . I am a
SUPERHERO.

And, funnily enough, being **SUPER** is not even slightly super. It's the OPPOSITE of super. It's actually super *un*-super.

What I mean is . . . I am not keen on it AT ALL.

For starters, even though I AM allowed to decide how I defeat **EVIL BADDIES** (even if I REALLY don't want to because I would much rather be at a **ROLLER DISCO** or reading a book), I'm NOT allowed to decide what clothes I wear. This is because my **mum** (yes, my **MUM**) picked them out for me already, and they are this . . .

. . . and I have to wear them all the time. FOREVER.

EYE ROLL

And while I am on constant alert and have to *dash* off at a moment's notice to save the planet, I still have to get my homework done on time.

Also, if I get accidental lunch spillage on my cape, I am in **BIG TROUBLE**, but if a super baddie like **MEGAVOM** throws up all over me, well, that's JUST FINE.

It's all just SO completely unfair.

Oh, and if I do mess up when I am doing all that . . . well, I don't want to worry you, but . . .

And, if I am being honest, it can get quite hairy sometimes. . . . For example, there was that time with **VOLTZ**. . . .

Then there was the time with

Harry the Slime. . . .

It always tends to work out because the rest of my whole, entire family is also **SUPER**, and we usually go on missions all together. Like a *fun family* day out, just with added baddies and minus the fun.

Anyway, that's pretty much how this **SUPER** business works—it doesn't tend to start with an insect bite/freak accident in a science lab/weather phenomenon. Oh no. You just get born into a family of **SUPERS** . . . and this is the bunch of weirdos I got born into. . . .

And even though I am saving the world

ALL

THE

TIME,

everyone at school still thinks I'm a total loser. Well, not quite **EVERYONE**. I mean, there's Ivy, **Ed**, and **Molly**, my friends and fellow **ECO COUNCIL** members. I know! Saving the world in AND out of school!

We've already sorted out some compost bins for the food waste in the cafeteria and made a wildflower corner next to the science hut (for bees and stuff), and that's just in one term. It's not exactly the same as having intergalactic battles with utter **SUPERVILLAINS**, but it's more fun, for sure. And there is the added bonus that I don't have to use my completely ridiculously awful **SUPERPOWER**, so that's good. What **IS** my **SUPERPOWER**, you ask?

Embarrassing. That's what it is. Super, SUPER embarrassing.

The bit where Perfecto arrives...

As it was Monday, I obviously had to go to school, and as it was Monday, I obviously found it EXTRA hard to get out of bed. "Lucky" for me, **WANDA** came to "help." . . . She **jumped** on my chest, which I just about managed to ignore, but when she started licking my face (and I am almost certain she had just eaten her extra-**STINKY** breakfast biscuits), I couldn't help but **leap** up and **scream** slightly.

Then **WANDA** told me we had to—go on a mission . . . RIGHT

THEN . . .

GREAT.[*]

WHIFFY

*Not great. Not even slightly.

BIG OLD BABY GOOGOO IS CAUSING CHAOS IN THE BIG CITY WITH HIS BRAND-NEW TOY... A GIANT REMOTE-CONTROL TEDDY BEAR....HE MUST BE *STOPPED!*

THE GIANT TEDDY IS STOMPING ABOUT ALL OVER THE PLACE... NAUGHTY BABY!

It's not often that having to get up really early on a Monday morning to fight a giant teddy controlled by a **SUPER BADDIE** dressed as a baby puts me in a good mood, but on this occasion it did, so I didn't even do a tiny moan about having to go straight to school. When I got there, everyone was so EXCITED—it felt all **jittery**, like it might be the holidays or something. But as it wasn't even slightly December, I knew it definitely wasn't that. I found Ivy in our study hall and asked her what on earth was going on. Ivy said she had no idea and, anyway, what was I talking about? Then I noticed she had her nose in the new **LLAMA-DRAMA-ARAMA** book, and I shuddered because it reminded me of the time I was hit on the head with a **LLAMA**. (I ALMOST feel ready to talk about it, but not quite.) Anyway, once Ivy has her head in a book, the world could actually blow up and she wouldn't even notice. Well, not unless the book got blown out of her hand.

LLAMA-DRAMA-ARAMA

So instead I asked **Molly**, who **ALWAYS** knows what's going on, and this time was no different. She told us that everyone was all **ajitter** because there was going to be a school **talent show**!!! I said, **"NO WAY!"** and **Molly** said, **"YES WAY!"** and there was even an actual poster about it up on the noticeboard by the main door. I said, was she sure it was a real poster and not a phony, like the one **RiCKY OWeNS** put up saying that the very next day was "dress up as a fruit day" for charity?

Result: lots of confused bananas and teachers the following day and **BIG TROUBLE** for RiCKy oWens **FOREVER**.

But **Molly** said she was sure it was the real thing, as this time it wasn't written in felt-tip and it had loads of pictures of kittens on it. This was a dead giveaway that actual Mrs. Fuller, who works in the office, made the poster. (She LOVES kittens.) . . . Hmmmmm, so it MUST be true.

LLAMA-&
DRAMA-
ARAMA

On the way to our first lesson we walked extra slowly past the poster, and it DID look real and official with lots of pictures of kittens with **"TALENTS"** all over it. (Though I am not sure what talent the picture of a kitten and a watermelon referred to, I had to admit the kitten painting at an easel was cute.) Everyone in the grown-up half of school was invited to do something for the show, if they wanted.

What a morning! I felt quite a bit excited, and I wasn't entirely sure why, as I don't have any obvious talents. I did like the idea of a **talent show**, though, and so did Ivy. We talked about it all day and felt that the **ECO COUNCIL** should definitely do something together, but what? I suggested we all meet up at the entrance to the park next to school later and have a chat about it . . . but just as the bell rang for the end of the day, there was **WANDA** . . .

AGAIN. . . .

WHAAAAAT?!?! . . .

Once I had wriggled out of the giant and not at all embarrassing*chocolate wrapper, I sat down, completely dazed, and quite a bit confused, and tried to work out what had just happened. (Oh, hang on, that was it . . .

I had been **totally defeated** by an

EIGHT-AND-A-HALF-YEAR-OLD.)

*actually completely embarrassing

I suddenly realized why **Perfecto** was called **Perfecto**. I mean, when you think about it, it's obvious, right? But I didn't think about it, so . . . I guess that's why my name ISN'T **Perfecto**.

The bit with Aunty Fury . . .

. . . shhhhh, don't tell anyone . . .

While I am used to being a loser at school, when I'm a **SUPERHERO**, I am usually on the winning side. Sometimes I might get covered in vomit or **STINK** juice or slime or whatever, but I always save the day. Well, WE always save the day. But now that I was on my own, I was LOSING to a **SUPER BADDIE** who is LOADS younger than me. Really?

I started to wonder who this **Perfecto** pip-squeak was, anyway. How come I had never heard of her before? I needed to know more and wondered who I could possibly ask. Then suddenly I realized . . . **Aunty Fury** might know something, what with her and **Perfecto** both being **SUPER BADDIES**. . . . Maybe she would be able to give me some **top secret,** super-villainous inside information in case I came up against **Perfecto** again. Obviously I had to visit **Aunty Fury** in total and complete secret, as I am not allowed to even talk about her, let alone pop in to see her. . . .

About two million (or maybe fifteen) years ago, **Aunty Fury** and **Granny** had the biggest fight EVER, and she decided then and there to be a right proper *BADDIE*. I have tried and tried and tried to find out what the argument was about, but **Mum** tells me to ask **Dad**, and **Dad** won't say a word. And I'm waaaaaay too scared to ask **Granny**, as even though she is a goodie, she definitely has *BADDIE* vibes.

Anyway, nowadays **Aunty Fury** spends her time trying to be the world's baddest *BADDIE* and mainly not quite managing it. But she does give it a jolly good go.

BADDIE *VIBES!!*

When I arrived at **Aunty Fury's** lair (which is basically a house for baddies), she was furious to see me, which was totally unsurprising because, well, she's called **Aunty Fury**. Once she had calmed down, she

told me off for visiting as she knew I was not at all allowed to and **Dad** would be cross with me. I reminded her she was a **BADDIE**, so why did she care? And then she was furious all over again.

Aunty Fury stopped shouting long enough for me to ask her about Perfecto, and it turned out she actually had quite a lot to say on the subject. . . .

DID YOU KNOW ONE OF THE MANY REASONS I GOT OUT OF THE SUPERHERO GAME WAS SO I DIDN'T HAVE TO BE PERFECT? YOU KNOW, LIKE YOUR AUNTY BLAZE.

AND, REALLY, HOW CAN YOU HAVE A BADDIE CALLED PERFECTO? I MEAN, IT JUST DOESN'T SOUND EVIL ENOUGH. OR EVEN SLIGHTLY BAD... RIDICULOUS!

EYE ROLL

(AHHH, SO THAT'S WHERE I GET IT FROM!)

But infuriatingly, **NONE** of the things she had to say were at all helpful!

Errr, thanks, Aunty!

FINALLY . . .

When I got back home and snuck in through my bedroom window (flying is extremely useful for this), I decided to call Susie, my friend from my old school in my old town, because she always says the right thing. Well, nearly always . . . that time she said I should let her crimp my hair was definitely NOT the right thing, but other than that, she is usually spot-on.

Susie told me about how she and Tom (my other best friend from my old school) had been on a school trip and bought matching sun visors in the shop after, and even though it made me a bit sad as I knew that if I still went to that school, I would have a matching visor too, it was really nice to hear their news. After that we discussed the **talent show** at great length, and we tried to work out how I could build my **ROLLER-SKATING** skills into the **ECO COUNCIL'S** performance. Then I told Susie about **Perfecto** and how I had been quite definitely beaten by an **EIGHT-AND-A-HALF**-year-old. Susie told me that

I shouldn't worry too much as **Perfecto** wasn't **THAT** much younger than me. And maybe that particular battle was more **Perfecto's** thing and not so much mine. And MAYBE I should just let it go because no one can win them all. And maybe I would never even have to see her again EVER. And I knew she was mainly right but somehow, SOMEHOW, I had a feeling this WOULD happen again. MAYBE, sometime in the dark and distant future, **Perfecto** and I would do battle once more, and maybe that would be my chance to defeat her. . . .

. . . Or maybe it would happen the next morning, before breakfast, which everyone knows is THE most important meal of the day, and I am almost certain that my missing it was entirely to blame for what happened next. . . .

Probably . . .

The bit where we form a band . . .

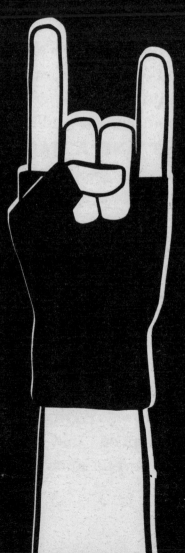

JETT and I sat outside the Stationery Superstore, feeling pretty dazed, and sort of stared at the sky that **Perfecto** had just disappeared up into. Had that really happened . . . **AGAIN**?

I looked at **JETT**, who shrugged her shoulders and swooshed her amazing sports hair back into place. I started to tell **JETT** all about **Perfecto** and how she was **ONLY EIGHT AND A HALF** years old but already a supergood *SUPER BADDIE*, and all while she was basically just a tiny baby. . . . It didn't make sense.

JETT said maybe it was because she trained hard, ate healthily, and had a positive mental attitude. But then **JETT** would say that, because she is an athlete and wins lots of prizes because she does all those things. I pointed out that there was being good at something and trying hard, and **THEN** there was **PERFECTO**.

JETT just replied that you couldn't always win, everyone knew that, she was quite simply the better super that day, and anyway, Coach said we should look at every defeat as a chance to learn. . . . I told **JETT** that this was actually the second time Perfecto had defeated me in two days, and then **JETT** did look a bit sad for me, but quickly smiled and said, in that case I should look at it as two chances to learn. But I had only learned one thing from both battles, that thing being that Perfecto was perfect and I, quite obviously, was **NOT**.

WOBBLY

EYE ROLL

LATER . . .

As I sat in the back of **Dad's** car on the way to school (unsurprisingly, my humiliating defeat had made me run a bit late—even less perfect), I couldn't shake the horrible feeling that I was going to get pummeled by this pint-sized *SUPER* again. And soon.

But how was I supposed to defeat the PERFECT *SUPER BADDIE*?

What was her secret?

Did I need to be more like JETT about the whole super thing?

So far I'd just sort of done my own thing **SUPERHERO**-wise . . . but was that enough? Was I being too relaxed about this whole saving-the-world business? Did I need a coach, like **JETT**? Or maybe I needed a plan . . . a Perfect **Perfecto** Plan!

When I got to school, I tried to talk about it with Ivy, but she just said that in our own ways we are all SORT OF perfect, like perfectly ourselves. I kind of think that was her way of trying to make me feel a bit better about being a **LOSER**. Then we both remembered that we still needed to sort out our entry for the **talent show** . . . . What were we going to do?

I suggested we should each make a list of the things we were good at, and then we could see if there was anything we were ALL good at. **Ivy** thought that was actually a great idea—**RESULT**! So we whispered it to **Ed** and **Molly**, who gave it the thumbs-up too. We agreed we would write our lists that morning and compare them over lunch.

LATER THAT DAY . . .

I really,
really,
REALLY
thought as hard as I could about what things I was good at, especially during physics, which sadly won't be going on my list. (I honestly do try, but I think the "egg incident" put me off a bit—another long story.) By lunchtime my list was looking quite short. Fortunately, everyone else's was too, well, except Ivy's, but then **Molly** remembered that I could burp the alphabet, and I remembered that **Ed** could click his toes, and **Ed** remembered that Ivy could do an impersonation of **Mrs. Wiggin** (the evil lunch lady), and Ivy remembered

Molly could touch her nose with her tongue. Then we spent at least ten minutes adding things to one another's lists. I am not really sure how helpful it actually was, but it was nice and it made me think about how it's much easier to think of things other people are good at than things you are good at. When we had all finished, we each had quite an impressive number of things we were good at . . . **YES!**

Sadly, none of the things on our lists matched. So there was nothing else for it.

ED

EATING COOKIES

BALANCING ON ONE LEG

DAYDREAMING

JUGGLING

DANCING

BUILDING CAMPS

COUNTING STUFF

COLLECTING
BUBBLE GUM

MOLLY

NOTICING THINGS
PAINTING
CHATTING
MAKING GREAT CARDS

FASHION STUFF

SLEEPOVERS

RUNNING
CATCHING

MATH

IVY

READING

WRITING

BIOLOGY

ORGANIZING

RECYCLING

IMPERSONATING OWLS

MAKING CAKES

HAVING WHAT YOU NEED
WHEN YOU NEED IT

REMEMBERING STUFF

PIZAZZ

FLYING

SAVING THE WORLD

TELLING JOKES

EATING PIZZA/DOUGHNUTS

HAVING COOL HAIR

MAKING PEOPLE LAUGH

DOODLING

PAINTING NAILS

We would just have to . . .

Well, this was beyond exciting. I had always wanted to be in a band and was very pleased that we weren't letting the fact that almost none of us actually played any musical instruments stop us! But first things first: What would we be called? We decided that, as this was the most important part of the band-making process, we could not rush it. We would all have a good long think and meet up after school to swap name ideas.

Then I saw **JETT** and ran over because I wanted to talk to her about **Perfecto** a bit more, swap strategies and all that sort of stuff. The sort of stuff I had never even thought of doing before, but something about **Perfecto** was really getting to me. Maybe it was the two

EYE ROLL

extra-embarrassing defeats I had suffered at her hands. Or it was quite possibly the fact that she was perfect, which made me feel like I definitely wasn't. Maybe. I mean, I had never really thought about myself as perfect, or even not-perfect, before, but this annoying villain was making me think all sorts of new and not-ever-so-nice things. When I told JETT all this, she just told me I could only do my best.

ERRR, OKAY, JETT, but clearly my best isn't good enough. So NOW what do I do? I have been utterly defeated not once but twice by a silly baby **SUPERHERO** who just happens to be straight-up flawless. How does doing my not-so-great best help with that?

Hmmmmm?

EYE ROLL

I did loads more thinking all afternoon. Unfortunately, it wasn't even slightly the sort of thinking I was supposed to be doing—I was thinking about band names during PE (which might explain the basketball in my face), I was thinking about **Perfecto** during math (which might explain me getting a sum wrong), and I was thinking about math during English (which everyone knows isn't at all useful). And I was so busy with all my thinking, I didn't even notice **Serena** teasing me the whole time, so I guess it wasn't completely bad.

But when the bell FINALLY rang for dismissal, I had only thought of a few band names, and I was almost certain none of them were very good.

AFTER SCHOOL . . .

I found **Ivy**, **Molly**, and **Ed** by the school entrance and was almost nervous to show them my band names. **Ivy** had three, **Molly** had one, and **Ed** had forgotten he was in a band. We put all the names into one not-very-long list and took a vote. It was unanimous, our band would be called . . . **The Cheese Squares.**

Serena and **The Populars** were obviously listening in on our conversation (**Serena** is SOOOOOO super popular I really do wonder why she spends so much time looking for things to tease me about. Surely she has better things to do.) and started laughing hysterically about our band, or **"STUPBAND,"** as **Serena** called it. I tried to point out that that didn't even make sense (I think she meant something about it being a stupid band???), but I gave up when I remembered that didn't matter because **Serena** had said it and everyone would just think it was hilarious anyway. Which, of course, they did.

As I wandered home, my annoying little sister, RED DRAGON, was jabbering away, so I used my tried-and-tested trick of stuffing my pigtails in my ears. . . . Ahhh, peace and quiet. Then I had a lovely time imagining the **stratospheric**, supersonic **SOAR-away** success of The Cheese Squares, and I realized that while today had been completely not-amazing in many ways

(my humiliating defeat before breakfast, JETT being totally unhelpful, Serena and The Populars finding The Cheese Squares HILARIOUS, and absolutely NO progress being made on my Perfect Perfecto Plan), it had been quite **AMAZING** in one way . . . I had started it not at all in a band and finished it in The Cheese Squares!

LATER THAT EVENING . . .

As I was sitting at my desk, or possibly lying on my bed, trying to do my homework but mainly feeding BERNARD (my soul mate and pet guinea pig) cool-ranch chips, I heard something hit my window. First I ignored it, but then it happened again and then AGAIN, and eventually I got up to see what on earth it was. It turned out it was *actual* earth, as KAPOW was throwing handfuls at my window and had just thrown one as I opened the window, which resulted in a face full of mud for me. **GREAT.**

And why couldn't he just have hovered up and knocked on my window like a normal *SUPER*? Well, a normal *SUPER BADDIE*. You see, KAPOW is actually my super-secret, *SUPER-BADDIE* best friend. **I KNOW!** We've known each other forever, though, and can't really see why being on opposite sides should spoil a perfectly good friendship. And, anyway, no one can make me snort-laugh like KAPOW.

We sat on my bedroom floor and ate the rest of Bernard's chips and giggled and giggled until KAPOW asked me about my day, at which point I stopped giggling, on account of my day having been quite lousy. I told KAPOW about Perfecto, and it turned out that KAPOW actually knew her from the super-evil-baddie-kids party circuit (yeah, they have one too), and he confirmed everything I suspected . . . Perfecto was **SUPER** annoying AND pretty perfect . . .

UGH.

After **KAPOW** had told me all that, I told him all about the two **COMPLETELY AWFUL** battles I'd had with *Perfecto*. **KAPOW** tried really, really hard not to laugh at this bit but failed quite spectacularly, which I know is not ever so kind, but he IS a **SUPER BADDIE**, so it's not all that surprising. But he did stop laughing when he saw how glum I was about *Perfecto*. I mean, he's not EVIL. Then I told him I was practically certain we would be doing battle again because **Perfecto** clearly had it in for me, so I was really, really, **REALLY** trying to come up with a Perfect **Perfecto** Plan to defeat her once and for all.

Because he is my best friend first and a baddie second, **KAPOW** brilliantly suggested we should go and spy on her for ideas, and he was almost certain he could remember where she lived from her eighth birthday party. . . .

Once we eventually found **Perfecto's** lair, we hovered up to the window with all the shiny trophies on the windowsill, because *of course* that was bound to be **Perfecto's** room, but when we peeked in, we realized

it completely wasn't. Inside we saw a sort of bigger and shinier version of **Perfecto**. . . . WHAT?!? This was all very confusing. . . . Well, it was until **KAPOW** told me it wasn't a **Perfecto** factory (my first thought), but it was actually **Perfecto's** big sister.

Just watching this **Perfecto** Version 2.0 made me and **KAPOW** feel exhausted, and we were about to go and take a nap when actual **Perfecto** burst into the room. She looked all different, not her normal know-it-all self. She was **bobbing** about trying to get big **Perfecto's** attention, but it didn't

really seem to be working, and she was trying EVERYTHING. Then her mum came in (I knew it was her mum as **KAPOW** let out a whimper—she's quite scary, even at birthday parties, apparently) and barked at **Perfecto** to leave her sister alone as she was busy *improving* herself. So she did.

KAPOW and I hovered around to **Perfecto's** actual window, which didn't have nearly as many trophies on it (I would still have been happy with them, though), and watched her looking miserable as she dusted her rosettes.

I didn't understand. Surely

Perfecto's sister

couldn't

be more

perfect

than

Perfecto?

I mean, she was perfect!!! Then **KAPOW** told me her sister was called **X-TRA**, as in like everyone else but MORE, and I almost felt sorry for **Perfecto**. I mean, did I know what it was like to have an annoying, better-than-me-at-everything sister? Errr, yes. But then I remembered that I didn't take it out on innocent **SUPERHEROES** with stupid, long capes and felt a bit cross all over again.

The bit where I become perfect . . .

I am used to waking up to a **SMELLY**-breathed dog/messaging service, and that is annoying, but my super-irritating little sister being the first thing I heard was just SUPER annoying.

And she was talking nonsense. . . . Apparently someone called Fenella was on the actual phone (not the **WANDA** phone) and wanted to talk to me about our science project because she wanted to make sure it was **PERFECT**! Well, errr, I don't know ANYONE called Fenella, and I am almost certainly NEVER going to do a science project perfectly, but as RED was clearly itching for me to explain everything to her, I just pretended I knew exactly what was going on and went, "Oh right," and marched off to the phone.

I should have guessed (and might have if I hadn't JUST woken up) that it wasn't actually Fenella, whoever she is, but in fact my **Aunty Fury** trying to be sneaky. . . . She had apparently done a bit of nosing around and confirmed my suspicions about the

super-annoying,

super-perky,

super-together

SUPER-BADDIE

Perfecto. . . . .

By the time I FINALLY got to school, Ivy had already decided we should have our first proper band rehearsal at lunchtime, and while that was fine by me, I did wonder how we would rehearse if we didn't know what we were playing, both song-wise and, more importantly, instrument-wise. But as being in an ACTUAL BAND was so exciting, I decided not to worry about that too much. All of us gulped down our lunches and headed to the music room for some inspiration.

Miss Cass, the music teacher, was there and was VERY enthusiastic about our band idea. Apparently, she used to be in a band at school called

MEGAROCKNOISEDEATH

(all one word), which wasn't the type of band I would have imagined Miss Cass to be in. Then she started to sing one of their songs, which was, erm, well, **LOUD**, and it all made perfect sense.

Once Miss Cass got down off the table and stopped singing/screeching, she was very helpful and agreed that I should probably play the guitar because it really worked with my overall "look." Ivy was Grade 4 piano, so OBVIOUSLY she would be playing the keyboard, and **Molly** was **EXTREMELY** excited about the idea of playing the drums, which just left **Ed**, who wasn't at all sure what he wanted to play. Then he saw the maracas.

While deciding which instruments we were going to play had been surprisingly easy, playing them was quite a bit **TRiCKiER**. This was strange because I had imagined myself playing the guitar so many times that I sort of thought I could. Unfortunately, this was definitely **not** the case. Of course Ivy was **GREAT** at the keyboard, but I wasn't sure *Beethoven* was our band's musical vibe. **Molly** was SUPER keen on the drums, which seemed to please Miss Cass loads. And **Ed** declared he was a natural at the maracas.

Even so, we all agreed that we could use some more practice before the **talent show**, and Miss Cass was super helpful about it all; she even said we could use the music room and instruments any lunchtime we liked and maybe even after school too, so long as we checked with her first.

The Cheese Squares were on their way to the school **talent show** (definitely) and global music domination (probably). **HOORAY!**

The rest of the afternoon went by in a bit of a **blur** as I was still very much enjoying my excitement about being in a band. This time on the walk home after school I was extremely busy imagining **The Cheese Squares'** first world tour, and I was just enjoying our third imaginary encore when I suddenly found myself in the flower bed at the front of our house. I wasn't entirely sure how I ended up there, and I was just about to blame the **LLAMA AGAIN** (SUCH a long story), but then I heard the calm and soothing* voice of **WANDA** with another mission. . . .

*not at all calm or soothing

I stomped into the house to the bathroom and washed off all my "toppings." And the ice cream. **UGH.** ENOUGH WAS ENOUGH! Annoyingly, tears were prickling my eyes, and I couldn't be sure if they were angry ones or sad ones. I marched off to find **WANDA**, to ask her why, oh why, oh why, oh why, oh WHYYYYYYYYY did she keep sending me off on missions to get completely beaten by the know-it-all-baddie-two-shoes-girly-nerd that is **Perfecto**? It was embarrassing and horrible and—oh yes—why did **Mission Control** just completely **HATE ME**?

WANDA looked at me, sniffed her paw, tried to scratch her ear, and walked away. As I yelled, "THANKS A LOT," after her, my double, triple, infinity annoying little sister, RED DRAGON, flick-flacked into the room. She smiled at me in a way that sort

HA! HA! HA! HA

of suggested she felt sorry for me (erm, no, thanks. If ANYTHING I should feel sorry for *you* for being such a loser . . . who wins everything . . . whatever) and suggested I play **Perfecto** at her own game.

I started to consider this, and then **RED** burst into laughter, and I realized she was joking. This was all very strange as that is exactly the sort of hilarious thing I say to **RED**, who is usually really nice and helpful and not at all sarcastic. I felt annoyed and proud of her all at the same time, which was very confusing. Well, ha-de-HA-HA, VERY funny, it's obviously COMPLETELY hysterically funny to imagine me triumphing over **Perfecto** by being as perfect as her. . . . Hmmmmmm, just imagine. . . .

HMMMMMMMM!

LATER THAT AFTERNOON . . .

Maybe **R ED'S** "joke" wasn't so funny, after all. Maybe that's exactly what I should try to do. **YES!** THIS was the Perfect **Perfecto** Plan, and thinking of it was quite possibly the start of me being actually fully perfect. Now I just had to be perfect in every other single way. . . . Easy. . . .

HA! I'd show this pesky terror **Perfecto** who was perfect around here!

FIVE MINUTES LATER . . .

Well, maybe it wasn't **THAT** easy, but surely I'll get the hang of it eventually.

TWO HOURS LATER . . .

That's better. In fact, that is **PERFECT**!

The bit where Bernard gets fed up . . .

I was so excited about being the brand-new and **PERFECT** me that I woke up super early the next morning, even before the sun had woken up. Even before *anyone* had woken up. There was just SO MUCH to do, so many things I had to be perfect at, SO MANY THINGS, it made me feel a bit panicky. But I told myself that perfect people didn't think like that (they were probably too busy being perfect—duh!) and wondered if maybe I should get up before the sun EVERY DAY to fit all the new perfect things in.

I went to get Bernard, who was fast asleep. Well, she was until I woke her up and told her all about me being **PERFECT**. Bernard is such a good listener and really gets me, which is why I was so surprised when, after I told her my plan, she looked at me like I had just said I liked beef-flavored chips or something. (We both agree they are the absolute WORST—UGH.)

Hmmm, maybe she hadn't understood? I mean, she is a guinea pig, so I explained it all again, and she still looked completely disgusted. What? It was the **PERFECT Perfecto** Plan! Was it just too confusing for her because—**NO!**—she wasn't perfect? Oh dear, poor Bernard. I really hoped this didn't mean I had to get a new and actually perfect pet. . . .

After a perfectly healthy (but completely disgusting) breakfast, I went to school and arrived perfectly on time. Ivy looked super surprised to see me so early, and then looked even more surprised when I told her that The Cheese Squares should definitely practice every lunchtime and after school until the **talent show**. I explained that we only had about a week and I *had* to be PERFECT, which therefore meant the band did too.

Ivy said that maybe we should just be as

good as we could be and have fun while we were doing that.

I pointed out that that sort of attitude wasn't going to win anyone anything, and Ivy then pointed out that it wasn't actually a competition, so I told her that, actually, maybe everything was a competition. And that today I had clearly won the most-perfect-hair-in-the-class competition.

Ivy asked how I could win a competition that no one else knew they were competing in, and I did an **EYE ROLL** because, really?

After an almost perfect (well, I had only just started) morning, I met Ivy, **Ed**, and **Molly** in the music room to rehearse. Once I'd given **Molly** a few pointers on her drum playing and **Ed** a couple of maraca tips, I tried to help Ivy with her keyboard business. I know I haven't played the piano for as long as Ivy, or even at all, but I felt she needed to tidy it up a touch and try to get it a bit more, well, perfect.

As we packed up, I told everyone that while they had tried really hard, The Cheese Squares should probably have as many rehearsals as possible because there was A LOT of room for improvement, and I'm pretty sure they all agreed. . . .

I had the **FIDGETS** all afternoon, as I realized halfway through attendance that I had been so busy "helping" everyone else in the band that I had forgotten to practice the guitar myself. And I really, really, REALLY needed A LOT of practice.

This made me feel quite Panicky as I wasn't sure there was time to go from zero to perfect with something as tricky as the guitar in just over a week, but not being perfect was no longer an option—I had my plan to think of.

I whizzed to the music room at dismissal, and Miss Cass very nicely said I could borrow the guitar if I was double careful. **HOORAY!** Now I could practice, practice, practice. . . . Proper *rock-and-roll* types didn't worry about sleep, did they? But then they didn't have homework and *SUPERVILLAINS* to fight too. Surely I could somehow manage it all . . .

perfectly.

Walking home, I felt that I had at least mastered carrying my guitar perfectly when I very nearly tripped over **WANDA**. Normally I would have gone FLYING, but instead I perfectly sidestepped her!

WHAAAAAATTTTTT?

My Perfect **Perfecto** Plan was WORKING!!!

Oh, it would be so nice to fall over less. . . . (Take that, **LLAMA**!)

WANDA looked disappointed, then told me to go and put the guitar away as I had a **mission** to go on. . . . **UGH!** I really didn't have time for a **mission**, unless I used this as a chance to practice my new perfectness?

It worked!
It
had
actually
worked.

I had beaten **ABOMINABLE** PERFECTLY.
Why hadn't I done this before?

Being perfect was **BRILLIANT**, and I
even gave **RED** some pointers on how to
defeat **BADDIES** on the way home. I think
she really appreciated them. Probably.
I told **Mum** I didn't have time for dinner
as I had to learn the guitar entirely (and
perfectly) and do my homework (also
perfectly), so she just made me a sandwich
(not **QUITE** perfectly, but I let it go).

DISAPPOINTING!

Once I got to my room, I practiced the guitar for hours and hours, but I STILL wasn't perfect, and that was starting to make me feel a bit **jittery**.

KAPOW popped by, which was very nice, but I really didn't have time for him or the **chocolate-covered maggots** he had brought with him (do perfect people eat chocolate? I hoped so) as I hadn't even started my homework.

KAPOW asked why I needed to be perfect at the guitar, and I started to explain everything, but then I realized I didn't really have time for all that, either.

KAPOW looked confused and said I was being really strange, not at all like myself. In fact, now that he came to think about it, I was being like **Perfecto**, or even worse, **Perfecto's** big sister . . . and why on earth would I do that? **KAPOW** said he thought that actually I was much nicer than either of them, and he should know because he had played them both at musical chairs.

HA! HA! HA! HA! HA! HA! HA!

THWOMP

I pointed out that while nice was all very, well, nice, it was by being PERFECT that I was going to defeat Perfecto. Which reminded me, I had work to do. . . .

Then KAPOW rolled his eyes (I think) and ZOOmed off. Ha! He was probably just jealous of my new (almost) perfection. Maybe.

As I jumping-jacked back to my desk (I didn't have a treadmill, so I had to make do), I caught Bernard giving me the STINK EYE. JEEZ, what was wrong with everyone? You'd have thought they would've been happy for me. I mean, I was very nearly PERFECT. But then I remembered I didn't have time to be thinking about all that, and I tried to play middle C.

Again.

And again.

And again.

The bit where the band split . . .

I was so tired I missed my first alarm and only managed one hour of guitar practice before school, which left me feeling ALL OUT OF SORTS. Then I accidentally ate an unhealthy breakfast, spilled a bit of it on my cape, and forgot my math book. I couldn't believe that that many things could go so completely wrong—and all before school.

UGH.

It just felt like there was SO MUCH TO DO and be better at, and I wasn't even slightly sure how I could manage it all.

Perfectly.

AT SCHOOL . . .

I went straight to the bathroom and had a jolly good chat with myself, SMOOTHED my almost-perfect hair down, managed not to even slightly cry (there was no time for that), and went to class. Ivy was super excited about The Cheese Squares, but she said that although she could practice at lunchtime, she couldn't make it after school.

Er, why? I asked Ivy what on **earth** was more important than making the band perfect. We couldn't possibly stand up in front of the WHOLE SCHOOL and not be perfect. I mean, how completely embarrassing—I had a reputation to maintain.

At this point Ivy raised her eyebrows, and I was about to say something hilarious back, but **Serena** butted in, cackling, saying something about me being the opposite of perfect, "like NOT perfect . . . hahahahaha."

REALLY?

I reminded **Ivy** that actually this was about defeating **Perfecto**, who clearly *was* perfect, and if she was, then I had to be too. And, anyway, why wouldn't you want to be perfect? I mean, really . . . PERFECT!!!!

Ivy looked exasperated and told me AGAIN (a little bit louder this time) that the **talent show** was about having fun, and then pointed out that I was actually making it the opposite of fun (or NOT FUN, as **Serena** would say) by trying to make **The Cheese Squares** perfect. That actually if we just enjoyed ourselves, everyone watching would enjoy it too.

Well, I couldn't help but  at this, because right now wasn't about enjoying myself—it was about being perfect! Hadn't she been listening to anything I'd been saying? Errr . . . **Perfecto**?!?!

And **Ivy** said that even she wasn't perfect. And I said, yeah, right.

GGGGGRRRRRRRRRNNRNNNHHHHHH

I tried, I really, really did, but I couldn't stop feeling a bit cross all morning about what Ivy had said about the **talent show** being fun. FUN? I mean, fun was fine, but I wanted to get it RIGHT. I could practice every hour until the show, but if the rest of The Cheese Squares didn't too, then what was the point? What with feeling a bit cross and trying to be perfect, I was completely exhausted by lunchtime. I wondered if I was just being a Wimp, and then I reminded myself it would all be worth it when I defeated Perfecto. I wasn't exactly sure at this point how my newfound perfection would defeat her, but I imagined it was all just a state of mind, and my mind was definitely in a right state.

Brilliant.

I met the rest of **The Cheese Squares** in the rehearsal room because I couldn't have lunch with them on account of having to do my French homework again because it wasn't QUITE perfect. Or should I say, *parfait*.

I could tell **Ivy**, **Molly**, and **Ed** were trying very hard, but it wasn't perfect. After I tried as nicely as I could to tell them this, **Ed** put down his maracas and said that he didn't want it to be perfect. None of his favorite bands were perfect, and apparently the

only reason he'd agreed to do the **talent show** was because he thought it would be a laugh and it definitely wasn't, so he was sorry to say he was going to have to leave the band.

Molly put her drumsticks down and said she felt the same as **Ed**.

I looked at Ivy, who shrugged her shoulders and said she had to agree with them. Ivy said that while it was obviously very tough having to fight a *BADDIE* called Perfecto, that didn't mean I had to become EXACTLY like her, and it definitely didn't mean The Cheese Squares did. She added that, in actual fact, she, **Ed**, and **Molly** thought I was already pretty perfect, Pizazz-wise. That's why they were my friends in first place.

Well, that was very nice. I mean, it really was, but it took Ivy ever such a long time to say it all, and if I was now a solo act, I really didn't have the time for so much chitchat. . . .

I had a lot of practicing to do. There was only a week till the show, and it was such a relief it was the weekend. . . . I would have ALL THAT EXTRA TIME to practice without school getting in the way. But one week wasn't really very long, plus Perfecto could attack at any moment. And

I HAD

TO BE

READY. . . .

BUT THEN, ON WEDNESDAY . . .

I ran out of school as soon as the bell rang. I passed Ivy and **Molly** in the hall, and I did want to stop and talk and try to make things right—I had been meaning to all week—but there just wasn't the time. I had to get home as soon as I could; there was still so much to do. . . .

I had just done my chemistry homework (twice), repainted my nails (no smudges), learned some extra French verbs (just in case), practiced the guitar (two new chords mastered—yes!), and I was about to straighten my hair (again), do my math homework (twice, possibly three times), ask **Mum** to start ironing my socks (it's a bit embarrassing she doesn't already, I mean, come on . . .), make a scale model of the human nervous system (I was hoping for some extra credit in biology), and learn the other 4,623 guitar chords, when

WANDA padded in, eyed me suspiciously, and told me I had a **mission** to go on.

REALLY??? Couldn't someone else do it? I DIDN'T HAVE TIME. It was like no one else could see all the hundreds and thousands of things I had to do and do and do again—it felt quite never-ending. Then **WANDA** butted in and told me the **mission** was against **Perfecto**, and I knew that this was the moment I'd been waiting for—my chance to *finally* beat her . . . **PERFECTLY.**

How?

How and why?

Why

and

how

and

why?

I had tried my best to do everything
perfectly, even on wheels, and I'd still lost.

The bit where I realize something super important...

I felt all discombobulated, sort of like I didn't even know what was perfect and what wasn't anymore. Not having any friends didn't feel perfect, but then being in a band "just for fun" didn't feel perfect either. I couldn't work out what to do, it was all so confusing and upside down.

After all this trying, my brain felt like the opposite of perfect. It just felt like a big jumble of EVERYTHING. And all of it made me feel quite lousy and a bit panicky and sort of sad, too.

I was in a total pickle and didn't know what to do with myself. I was trying so hard to be perfect, to be the perfect **SUPER** and beat **Perfecto**, but no matter how hard I tried, I didn't seem to ever be **perfecto** enough.

A SHORT FLIGHT LATER . . .

When I got home, **Aunty Blaze** was there, on her way home from some really important **Mission Control** business, and suddenly I felt myself getting really cross. She managed to do everything perfectly (even evil **Aunty Fury** said so), but then sent me off on missions where I would be completely thrashed and embarrassed and left feeling really stupid and useless. Why would she do this to me? Why would **Mission Control** do this to me?

Accidentally I said all these thoughts out loud, and now everyone was looking at me like I was even more of a loser than ever. **Mum** looked like she was going to tell me off, but **Aunty Blaze** stepped in and suggested we go for a walk and have a little talk.

Aunty Blaze said she'd been watching what had been happening, and while she did feel a bit bad, she also knew that this was an important part of being *SUPER*. According to her, all *SUPERHEROES* question themselves sometimes. Apparently it's actually a good thing, and so is learning from other people—it's how we become better *SUPERHEROES*. (I hear that this works for normals, too.)

But thinking we are completely awful and then trying to be just like someone else entirely is not so good. In fact, it's really very bad. *SUPER BAD*. It's even worse if we think that the person we want to become is perfect, because we could all run around like crazy FOREVER, trying to be just like them, and it wouldn't help one bit because there is NO SUCH THING as perfect.

So it turned out everyone was right after all. This should've made me feel better, but honestly it just made me feel **EVEN** more stupid and useless.

BUT Perfecto? How could Aunty Blaze explain her? She did EVERYTHING perfectly, which just made me feel worse and worse, and I didn't know how to stop.

Aunty Blaze reminded me again that NOBODY is perfect, not even Perfecto, and maybe the way to stand up to her was to try being **MY** best and not **HER** best.

And when Aunty Blaze explained it like that, it seemed really obvious. I asked her if *she* was perfect, and she actually snort-laughed and said she was far from perfect in many, many ways (I think the snort-laugh helped me believe that), and then she asked me if I remembered the time she cooked lasagna, and then I did remember and was a little bit sick in my mouth because . . .

EEEUWWWW

When we got back home, **Grandma** and **Gramps** had popped over. **Gramps** had heard that I was playing guitar in the **talent show** and wondered if I would like to borrow his guitar for good luck. Apparently some bloke called **Elvis** gave it to **Gramps** a million years ago (approximately) as a thank-you for saving him when he got stranded on the moon in a Cadillac. I'm not sure I believed the story, but—errr—**YES, PLEASE**!

I asked **Gramps** if he played the guitar himself and if he did, could he tell me everything he knew and fast! In fact, RIGHT NOW!

Gramps chuckled and said, of course, but I wasn't to worry too much about getting it exactly right. The important thing was to enjoy it, because there would always be more to learn. The trick, said **Gramps**, was to enjoy the ride.

Then **Grandma** rolled her eyes and said he was starting to sound like his old friend Jimi Hendrix, and I said, "Who?"

And **Gramps** rolled his eyes too, because, apparently, really?

Everyone stayed for dinner. **Dad** had made his new "signature dish"—chili—what a surprise.* As we all went to sit down, **Mum** told me off for leaving my schoolbag in the middle of the hall, **RED** told everyone about getting a hundred on her math test, and I *tripped* over my cape. Everything was back as it should be. It felt really good being myself again, not to mention much less worry-making.

When everyone had finally gone home, I went to see **Bernard** and explained the situation, and she didn't even slightly give me the **STINK EYE**, and she even seemed to really enjoy the little bit of guitar I played her—perhaps I *was* improving! But I couldn't help being a bit worried as I didn't have a Perfect **Perfecto** Plan anymore. I mean, even though I had finally realized **Perfecto** wasn't actually perfect, I still hadn't worked out how I could defeat her. Maybe a good night's sleep would help. Or maybe NOT . . .

* not even slightly a surprise

THE VERY NEXT DAY . . .

I raced into study hall FIRST THING. I think Ivy thought it was still me trying to be all perfect and she looked a bit scared, but when I explained everything to her and said sorry about a million times, she just looked happy. Which made me happy too. Then I was double happy when she agreed to come back into the band and even helped me convince **Molly** and **Ed** to give it another go. This was a bit tricky as **Ed** had had an offer from a rival band to be their maracas player (he had been practicing and was, according to **Ed**, very good now), but when I absolutely, completely, and solemnly promised that we would not be even slightly perfect but we would have lots of fun, he was IN!

The Cheese Squares
were back
together!

We practiced at lunchtime and after school, but not because we were trying to be perfect (there was very little chance of that)—we were just enjoying ourselves so much. I told everyone about the Rock'n'Rollas, and we came up with some **DAZZLING** ideas for our show. Miss Cass was very encouraging about our "staging" ideas and even shared some of the things she used to do when she was in

MEGAROCKNOISEDEATH

(all one word), but honestly, I don't think anyone wanted to see us in glittery unitards, and I had no idea how we would all get big perms before the show. We thanked her anyway, though.

DA, DA, DAAAAA . . .

The **BIG DAY** arrived. The **talent show** was in the Big Hall all afternoon, which was great for a few reasons. . . . We would miss physics, we would get to watch the other acts, and **The Cheese Squares** would do their first, and quite possibly last, ever performance! **Ivy**, **Molly**, and **Ed** all had their rock-and-roll makeup looks planned—of course I didn't need one as I spend my whole life wearing a mask **EYE ROLL**—but I did have my lucky **Elvis** guitar. None of us ate much lunch (not even **Ed**, and it was his favorite chocolate chip cookies for dessert) as we were just *fizzing* with excitement. And then the time finally came. . . .

SHOWTIME . . . .

Mrs. Harris, our teacher, was announcing all the acts, and I was so excited that not even **Serena** could make me feel bad about **The Cheese Squares** (but she did give it a very good go). She was in a band with **The Populars** called

The PONY CLUB PRincesses,

and they all sang in harmony, or very nearly. I had to admit they were actually pretty good, and of course everyone **loved** it because . . . **Serena!**

FINALLY . . .

It was our turn. We all walked onstage, looked at one another, and smiled, then **Molly** clanked her drumsticks together three times and we were off. . . . Things were going exactly as we had planned— it was **loud** and it was **fast** and we were having fun. At least we were until . . .

WELL, I HONESTLY DON'T REALLY KNOW WHAT THIS IS ABOUT NOW. OTHER THAN HEARING FROM MY FRIEND, A PEKINGESE CALLED RONALD, THAT PERFECTO'S MUM WAS A BIT MIFFED SHE LOST ONE OF THE ROLLER CHALLENGES. SO PERFECTO IS BACK, BACK, BACK TO SORT THIS ALL OUT, ONCE AND FOR ALL...
E TALENT SHOW IS N FULL SWING...
The Cheese Squares
ER, EXCUSE ME...YOU CALL THIS MUSIC???
YOU CAN'T EVEN PLAY THE INSTRUMENT PROPERLY.
BUT I CAN PLAY LOADS...
I CAN PLAY FLUTE...
I CAN PLAY CELLO...
...EVEN THE TUBA
TAKE YOUR PICK!

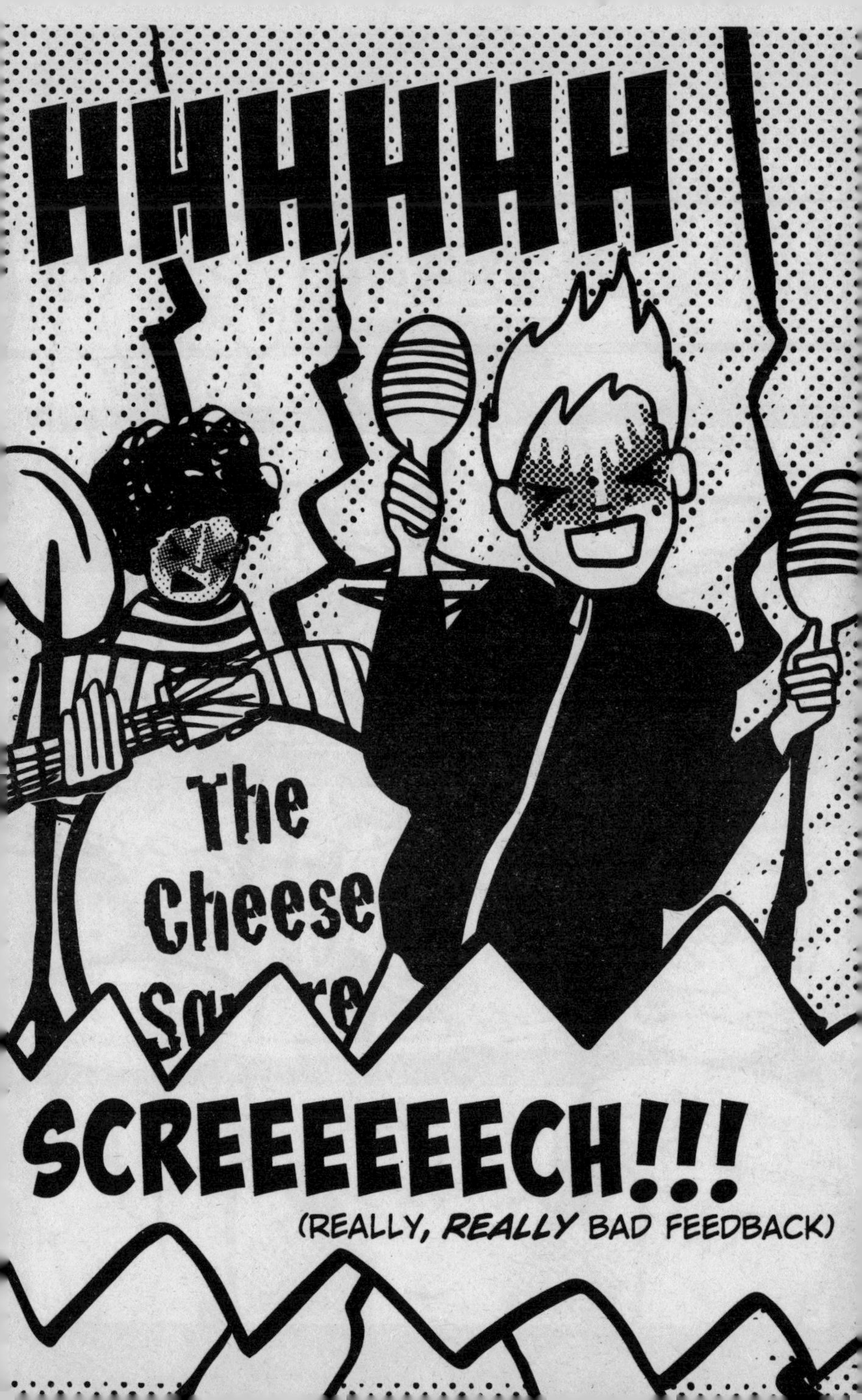
HHHHHH!
The Cheese
SCREEEEEECH!!!
(REALLY, *REALLY* BAD FEEDBACK)

I looked over at **Perfecto** and saw her all **CRUMPLED** and **CONFUSED**, and then I was confused too because I thought beating my first official **SUPER** nemesis would make me feel **GREAT**.

But it didn't.

It didn't at all . . . which is very confusing for a **SUPERHERO**, let me tell you!

Because now that I knew how completely horrible it felt to try to be perfect, and obviously not manage it, I actually felt a bit bad for **Perfecto**. She was trying to achieve the impossible all the time, and that must be **exhausting**. I should know. And, anyway, even before all this perfection madness, I got tired just trying to achieve the extremely possible.

I felt all my **crossness** at her for making me feel like a useless twit disappear, and instead I could see that this eight-and-a-half-year-old youngster could use some of my wise old wisdom, wisdom that can only come from being about a whole year older.*

* And also from having a helpful aunty, Gramps, and some pretty AWESOME friends. Possibly.

I wanted to tell her that no one is perfect. No one can be perfect, not even super-annoying little or big sisters, no matter how hard they try. And that actually when you are just trying to be perfect

ALL
THE
TIME,

you are missing out on all the good stuff, like fun and friends and enjoying what you are doing instead of worrying about it.

But that felt like it was A LOT all in one go, so instead I said I liked her new hairstyle, and she rolled her eyes (I know, I am just SUCH a trendsetter), and I said, no, really, it looked cool messy and that sometimes things were all the better when they weren't even SLIGHTLY perfect.

Then I told her I had spent all week trying to be just like her because I thought she was perfect, but I failed. But while I was failing to be perfect, I did realize I could only ever be me, and I definitely make mistakes, which I realized is actually a **great** thing because

sometimes our mistakes can actually turn into our biggest successes. You know, like being a surprise guitar rock god or getting a cool new messed-up hairstyle.

Perfecto gave a tiny smile and looked a teensy bit relieved but also a lot worried, and I thought that this would have to be a work in progress—she couldn't completely change just like that (and her name IS actually **Perfecto**—we'd have to have a think about that . . . IMPerfecto? Not-Exactly-Perfecto? **FURFECTO**? Which would have to involve a fluffy costume—CUTE!). So I handed her a tambourine and invited her to join in with **The Cheese Squares**' far-from-perfect performance.

First of all **Perfecto** said she couldn't as she had never played the tambourine before and what if she was no good? So I told her that if she wasn't very good, she would fit right in and that actually, as **Gramps** said, the trick is to enjoy the ride.

She even looked like she enjoyed it. Possibly.

The last bit . . .

I hadn't realized, but **Gramps** had snuck into the hall to watch us, and when it was finished, he said he didn't know how it could have gone any better.

Miss Cass agreed, and even **Mrs. Harris** said that it was a very spirited performance.

Then **Gramps** promised to take us all out for milkshakes to celebrate the beginning of **The Cheese Squares**' musical journey, and **Perfecto** said she'd try to come along but she was extremely busy generally improving in EVERYTHING.

I gave her what I hoped was a stern look, though just in case it wasn't, I made a mental note to tell **KAPOW** to visit her, as he is really very good at being a bit distracting and having fun.

Then **KAPOW** said he absolutely would, and I remembered that he is telepathic and told him to get out of my head RIGHT NOW, and he just laughed and told me to make him, so I thought of the worst possible thing ever (EVIL lunch lady **Mrs. Wiggin** serving up a plate of cooked liver, if you must know, UGH!), and he beat it.

And apparently **KAPOW** IS being very distracting, teaching **Perfecto** all the ways he enjoys being not perfect and having fun. She has won fewer trophies, but she smiles lots more. Especially for a **BADDIE**. Sometimes she even pretends to launch

an attack on a hair-bobble factory or something so I get called out to defeat her, but then we just sneak off for a catch-up and some chips. It's great. So now I have two *SECRET BADDIE* best friends, result!

THe PoNy CLUB PRinCesseS won the **talent show**, even though it wasn't even a competition, but honestly we didn't mind. We knew **The Cheese Squares** were probably just ahead of their time and that everyone would grow to realize what rock-star geniuses we all are.

Definitely.

Maybe . . .

Future rock genius Ed!

What we knew for sure was that we had all tried **OUR** best, not somebody else's best, but *our* best, and that was, in its own utterly imperfect way . . . kinda perfect.

I KNOW!!!

Confusing, isn't it?

Oh well.

The End . . .

Check out my other adventures!
Pizazz and
Pizazz vs. the New Kid

Read all of Pizazz's *SUPER* adventures!

Looking for another great book?
Find it
IN THE MIDDLE.

Fun, fantastic books for kids
in the in-be**TWEEN** age.

IntheMiddleBooks.com

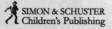